Office Misconduct

S.L. STERLING

Copyright

Office Misconduct

Copyright © 2021 by S.L. Sterling

living or dead, is entirely coincidental. Disclaimer: This book contains mature content not suitable for those under the age of 18. It involves strong language and sexual situations. All parties portrayed in sexual situations are consenting adults over the age of 18.

ISBN:

Editor: Brandi Aquino, Editing Done Write
Cover Design: Thunderstruck Cover Design

Brooke

I glanced around the empty halls of the office. Frank, my boss, had left only a few short hours ago, but I stayed behind to finish up the paperwork for his last meeting tomorrow morning. Hitting enter on my keyboard, I turned around and looked out over the city while I waited for everything to print. There was something so peaceful about New York from sixty-five stories up. There was no noise, no business, just a perfect view of the city that I rarely ever tired of, and of course, my thoughts.

I pulled the documents from the printer, stapled them together, and shoved them into the file folder that sat on my desk. Grabbing my sweater off the back of my chair, I wrapped it around me and sat back down to send Frank an email. The second I pressed send, I realized that after six long years of working side-by-side with Frank, this was going to be one of the last emails I ever sent to him. A wave of sadness fell over me at the thought.

Frank had just accepted a job in Texas six weeks earlier, and they had given him one month to wrap things up here. The second he had told me, I felt the tears building behind my eyes. He had been good to me, looking out for me when I'd first moved to New York and started with the company. He had been a dream to work for, but I was happy for him and his career move, even if it left me feeling sad and lost. To my surprise, a few days later, he told me he was working to negotiate a deal for me to accompany him to Texas to be his assistant. I knew they probably had far better assistants there than me, but he was insistent that he needed me. Two weeks later, he presented me with an amazing offer. I wanted to jump at the chance but kept a level head and asked for a couple of weeks to decide.

I'd walked into the office this morning with a heavy feeling weighing over me, and after dropping my purse and coat at my desk, I knocked on his door.

"Morning, Brooke. Come in," Frank greeted from his desk. *"I grabbed you a tea on my way in."* He nodded to the cup that sat on the corner of his desk.

I smiled, realizing how much I was going to miss that.

He brought me a tea every single morning, I doubted my new boss would be that way. "Thank you. Do you have a minute?"

"Of course." He shoved his paperwork to the side and nodded to the chair across from him. "This all can wait. What's going on?"

"I, uh, I've given your offer a lot of thought over the last couple of weeks."

"And?"

"Well, as generous as it is, I am going to have to pass. Andrew and I are going to give our relationship another chance and honestly, my heart is here in New York."

Frank set his pen down and looked at me, nodding. "Well, as sad as I will be to lose you, you need to do what is right for you. That much I understand," he said, smiling. "So I want you to always remember that if you change your mind, I am a phone call away."

"Thanks, Frank. I appreciate everything you have done for me."

"It's been a pleasure, and you're welcome. Now we need to start the day, which means you need to get to work. I have a lot of things I need before my meeting tomorrow," he said, smiling. "Oh, and don't forget your tea." He said leaning over and handing me the cup.

I went about my morning feeling good about my decision, and then I met Andrew for lunch over at the

Island Grill. Ten minutes after the food arrived at the table, his phone rang, and he spent the next fifty minutes on a conference call, leaving me to eat alone. He put his phone down long enough to pay the bill and kiss me good-bye before making his way back to the office. He'd sent me many text messages all afternoon, apologizing for not being present during our time together, promising to take me to dinner tonight to make up for it. Even though I was angry at him, I finally replied, agreeing to meet him, on the condition that he had finished work for the day and would spend quality time with me. Only then would I leave for the restaurant. I glanced at the clock and noticed it was almost eight. I knew that if I hadn't heard from him before now that he was going to break his promise of taking me to dinner.

I was about to move on to the next file that Frank had asked me to complete when my cell phone buzzed on my desk. I glanced at the screen. Just as I thought, Andrew was working late, something about an office emergency, and that he would just crash at his place tonight. My stomach sank and a tear slipped down my cheek, even though I already knew he would cancel. I allowed myself a couple of minutes to come to grips with the fact that I apparently cared more about this relationship than Andrew did, and knew that it would never work between us. I shoved my phone into my purse, downed a mouthful of coffee and buried my head back into the file I was working on.

It was after ten when I slid my key into the lock of my apartment and opened the door. I pulled my heels off, dropped my keys and purse on the table, and walked over to the window. I looked out over the city. I still preferred my view from my office window, but it still wasn't an unpleasant view from thirty-five stories. I flipped the lamp on in the room's corner, turned on the TV to drown out the silence, and headed to my bedroom to slip into my sweats. I was glad that Andrew was spending the night at his place. It had been a long day and I wasn't in the mood for him tonight. I pulled my hair back into a ponytail, brushed my teeth, and washed the makeup off my face. Once I was curled up on the couch, I quickly placed an order for delivery from The Spaghetti House. I'd had a craving for their eggplant parmesan all afternoon and couldn't wait to sink my teeth into it.

An hour later, I sat on the couch with my feet curled up underneath me. The last bit of my cold dinner sat in front of me on the table accompanied by the half empty bottle of wine I'd enjoyed while I watched the last two episodes of *Yellowstone* on my DVR.

I was about to head to bed when my cell phone

buzzed. I frowned. It was a little after one in the morning and I grabbed my phone, figuring it could only be Andrew or Sara. Instead, I sat there staring down at a name I hadn't seen in a couple of years come across the screen. What was Nate Templeton doing messaging me?

I sat there staring down at the only two words he had sent, "You up?" A funny feeling circled in the pit of my stomach at the thought of him sitting there waiting for my response. My fingers danced over the keyboard, typing out a response, then my finger hovered over the send button, only to chicken out and delete what I had written. I put my phone down. It would be a mistake messaging him. I didn't need feelings for someone I would never have creeping back into my life.

I turned everything off and headed to my bedroom, grabbing my book and crawling under the covers. I was halfway through a chapter when my phone vibrated gently against the table. I picked it up, looking down at the message. "Afraid to talk me?"

I laughed to myself. That was so Nate. I bit my bottom lip, held my breath as I typed out a response, and hit send.

"You look exhausted," Sara, my best friend of fifteen years, said as she walked along beside me. "New boss not working out?"

"It's not that. He hasn't even arrived yet." I shrugged.

"Then what is it? I mean, you are totally not yourself this morning. Look at you. I don't think you even ran a brush through your hair before throwing it up in that makeshift ponytail."

I blew out a breath as I walked beside her. We'd just finished a session of yoga and I felt no better than I had earlier. Normally, I'd feel so relaxed that I'd be ready for a nap, but not this morning. I'd called Sara in a panic because I hadn't wanted to be alone today. She immediately called in sick to work and told me to meet her in half an hour in Central Park for yoga.

"It's not the new boss, and I brushed my hair, thanks."

"Then what is it?"

I could feel the frustration building in me and knew I needed to get it all out. "It's Andrew," I huffed, "We had another fight last night. We are over. This time he stormed out of the apartment with his bag in hand and slammed the door behind him. I found my spare key on the kitchen counter after he left last night."

"Wow, I am so sorry, Brooke. I know how much Andrew meant to you, how hard you both were trying to make that relationship work," Sara said, throwing her arm around my shoulder to try to comfort me.

"To be honest, what's bothering me so much is that I don't really even feel that upset over the whole thing. It's been apparent for a long time that I was the one trying harder out of the two of us."

"Don't say that."

"No, I'm serious. I didn't even cry, Sara. He stormed out of the apartment, and I didn't even shed a tear— not one. I just curled up into bed and went right to sleep as if everything were fine."

"You didn't cry?"

"No. All that kept going through my mind was

worrying about the fact that I threw away a good career move because of him."

Sara looked at me, shocked at what I was saying. Andrew and I had been together for three long years. We'd even talked about getting married.

"What are you going to do now?" Sara asked, still shocked at the fact that I was more upset at losing out on Texas than I was about losing the man I had supposedly loved.

I stopped walking and turned toward her. "I also decided that I'm turning over a knew leaf."

"What would that be?"

"To be a little more spontaneous. I'm only twenty-eight. Who says I need to settle down? Perhaps I need to sew my oats, or wild oats, or whatever oats it is that people sew now."

Sara looked at me and we both burst out laughing. This was exactly what I needed after the way things ended last night—a walk through Central Park in the spring with my best friend, and laughter, lots of laughter.

"Well, that is a great idea, but I have a better one. Perhaps you need to stop being a workaholic and come out with your best friend for a night on the town. You'll never sew oats at work. Also, you need to get some other men out of your system first. Who was the guy you told me about from college? You know, the one who got away?"

"Who? Scott? He's married with two kids and a minivan."

"Was he the one that you wanted but never..." Sara raised her eyebrows at me in jest.

"Oh no, that was Nathan. Well, Nate."

"Perhaps you should call him or text him, see what he is up to."

Nate and I would hang out, have dinner and drinks, fool around. We were friends with some benefits, but something always impeded our relationship going further than that. On my part, I knew it was fear. I was so attracted to him, so consumed by him that I could barely understand what I was feeling.

After a while, we went our separate ways; however, we always kept in contact. I'd wanted to try again a couple of years later, but when I'd contacted him, he was dating someone. When that relationship ended and he contacted me, I was the one in the relationship.

When we were both finally single, I'd invite him over to my rarely ever empty dorm room, but he'd show up late. I would have already cracked a bottle of wine or just as he arrived my roommate would return, making it impossible for us to be alone together.

After college, we'd once again gone our separate

ways, keeping in touch only on holidays. We'd flirt innocently back and forth for a couple of days, but they were nothing more than just words on a screen. We were planning to get together three years ago for dinner, but a month before I met Andrew, and that dinner date never happened.

I shrugged my shoulders. I had thought about Nate often over the last month, we'd been texting almost daily, yet I'd mentioned nothing to Sara.

"You're insane. I'm not calling him. There is no way that he even remembers what happened between us," I somewhat lied.

"Oh come on! From what you've told me about the two of you, it sounds like he'd remember you."

"No, I doubt it," I said, pointing toward Better Beans on the corner. "Want to get a coffee?"

"That sounds great! They should have their new lattes out and their pumpkin scones ready by now, which I am dying to have," Sara said excitedly.

"We just finished yoga and now you want to eat sugar?" I questioned.

"Damn straight." She grabbed me by the elbow and pulled me over to the door of Better Beans, laughing all the way. "Besides, I saw the advertisement for those scones. I have been dying to have one. Every year at this time, I crave them. I can practically taste it now!"

I giggled and looped my arm through hers, and together we pulled the large doors of the small cafe open and stepped inside. The air was heavy with the scent of coffee and we both got in line to order.

"For real though, you should message him. I think he sounds like something you need right now," Sara blurted out to me as we stood in line.

"Who?" I asked, looking up from the email I was reading.

"God, you aren't that dense. Nate. You should message Nate!" she whispered, shoving into my shoulder, trying to peek down at my screen.

"What should I say? Hey, Nate, been thinking of you. Want to come screw?"

"Girl, no, feel him out," Sara said with a completely straight face and then burst into laughter. "I swear I didn't mean for it to come out like that, but text him, talk to him, see where his head is at. You never know."

I shrugged, feeling worse for holding back the fact that we had already been texting. "Can I tell you something?" I turned to her while the guy in front of me placed his order.

"Of course."

"Nate and I have been messaging for the past month."

"Get out of here. Seriously? And..." Sara said, her eyes lighting up as she waited for my response.

"There isn't much to tell. We keep it generic, just a 'hey, how's it going,' and once in a while, we talk about our day. Honestly, I know nothing about him. I don't know what he does for a living or if he's married or single."

"So what."

"So what? Are you suggesting that if he is married, I should pursue an affair with him? I am not that kind of girl. Just because I kept his number in my phone means nothing. Regardless, this is a stupid conversation. You know just as well as I do that I am not going to message him and do any of those things."

"So, you're admitting to me that you kept his number and that you keep in regular contact just because?" Sara giggled and reached into my jacket pocket, pulling out my phone.

"I wouldn't call one month out of five years regular contact, Sara."

She waved her hand in front of my face, dismissing my words. "If you won't text him, I will. Give me your password." She stood there with a goofy smile on her face, waiting for me to divulge my password. Instead I reached over and took my phone from her hand, placing it inside my other pocket.

"As I was saying, I wouldn't call it regular contact. I would call it, when we're bored, we talk. That's it. Besides, he lives over three hours from here. The last thing I would need is a long-distance relationship right now," I confessed.

"Excuses, excuses," she said, shaking her head as she handed me my cup.

"It's not an excuse."

"Then what is it? Besides, I thought you knew nothing about him?"

"I don't."

"You know that he lives three hours from here?"

I rolled my eyes at her, my cheeks flushing, as I lifted the lid off my coffee cup and dumped two sugars inside. I stood there trying to come up with a rebuttal but couldn't think of anything.

"Brooke? Brooke Summers, is that you?" a deep voice asked, interrupting us.

I froze as a chill ran threw me. I knew the voice anywhere. I turned around slowly and could barely believe my eyes. There in front of me stood the man we'd just been talking about. He looked the same as he did back in school. Same muscular build, same thick, dark hair that I longed to run my fingers through, and the same light-blue eyes that had mesmerized me from the first time I'd looked into them. I swallowed hard.

Nate had not changed a single bit, and I couldn't help but let my eyes wash over him.

"Nate? What are you doing here?" I swallowed hard, it was a stupid question, considering we were in a coffee shop, and immediately I felt my cheeks heat with embarrassment as Sara stood giggling beside me.

He held up his coffee cup and gently wiggled it back and forth. "Same as you it appears." He smiled and laughed.

"Right." I felt the heat rise to my cheeks. "That was sort of a stupid question," I said, wishing I could crawl into a small spot and hide.

Nate looked at me and smiled. I watched as his eyes danced over my body and back up to my face.

"Hi, I'm Sara," Sara said, shoving her hand out for him to shake. "Brooke's best friend. She was just talking about you."

"Oh really." Nate looked from Sara to me and smiled in question. "Care to enlighten me?" Nate said looking from Sara back to me.

At that moment, I seriously wished I hadn't said a word to Sara about Nate. I also wished that Sara had gone into work today like she was supposed to, instead of skipping out because I was having some sort of emergency life crisis.

"It was nothing," I bit out.

"No, I'm intrigued. What was it you were saying about me?" he asked with a glimmer in his eyes.

"I just mentioned you in conversation is all," I muttered.

"Yeah, just in conversation is all," Sara bit out, shaking her head, basically telling him I was lying. I elbowed her in the side, trying hard to get her to shut up.

"Well, Brooke, I'd certainly love to stay and chat, but I have to run. I have meetings to attend, but I'm in town for the weekend. I'm here for a couple more nights right now, staying at The Plaza, leaving Tuesday or Wednesday. Call me. You have my number. Perhaps we could have dinner and catch up."

I didn't say anything—I just kept my focus on his eyes—but when I felt Sara elbow me in the side, I nodded. "Sounds good."

"It was good to see you again, Brooke. Sara, it was nice to meet you," he said, not taking his eyes from mine. "Hope I hear from you," he said leaning in and kissing me on the cheek before turning and walking out of the cafe.

The entire sound of the coffee shop around me fell away as I watched him walk out the door of Better Beans. Then I felt Sara pull on my arm and squeal into my ear, "Oh my God, did you see how he just looked at you? He fucking wants you," she said, pulling me over to an empty booth, "You've got to call him."

I was still looking over at the door he had just walked out of as I sat down on the booth's soft seat.

"Don't be ridiculous," I said finally, pulling my eyes away from the door and looking over at Sara.

"I'm not being ridiculous. Jesus, the sexual tension between the two of you has me hot and bothered. You two would blow up an entire city block if you got together. Explosive. You've got to call him."

I shook my head and took a sip of my coffee. "He's the past, Sara. It's never a good thing to revisit your past. It didn't work the first time for a reason."

"Well, excuse me for saying so, but the past just fucked the crap out of you with his eyes while standing in a coffee shop, so I say you need to call him!"

I glanced at my best friend and gently smiled and shook my head. She did not know how badly I wanted to call, no idea how badly I wanted one more shot with that man. She also did not know how unsettled I felt deep down inside about the whole situation either.

I flung my suit jacket over the back of the chair and sat down at the desk, opening my laptop to respond to a few emails. It had been a long day of interviews and I was pleasantly surprised when I walked out of the last one to receive a phone call from Brixton Finance. I'd had an interview with them a week ago, and they called me this afternoon to offer me the position I'd applied for, and I'd accepted. I was now one of the top executives at Brixton Finance, complete with a corner office on the sixty-fifth floor, complete with my very own assistant, whom I had yet to meet. I'd felt lighter than I had in months.

"We will see you Monday. You'll be busy throughout the morning with meetings, but by the afternoon you should be able to get acquainted with your assistant."

"Sounds great, Ron. I look forward to it. I will need a couple of weeks to get an apartment and get settled in the city."

"That's fine. I will make sure that Brooke takes care of anything that might need immediate attention while you are away. She will also make sure you're kept up-to-date of anything that is important. Hell, she can probably even short list a few available apartments for you to look at."

"Brooke?" I asked.

"Yes, your assistant. Don't worry, Frank had nothing but glowing remarks about her."

I couldn't help but allow my mind to wander to this morning. Could it even be possible that it was her? Would fate be that cruel?

"I'm sure. Well, I look forward to meeting everyone. I will see you bright and early Monday morning."

"Perfect. I have sent you a few emails so please, as soon as you can, fill out the forms that are attached and send them back."

"Will do."

I took a few moments and responded to the emails he had sent, and then I headed to the bathroom for a hot shower. I had so much to do in such a short time, the first being to find an apartment, the second was to get Brooke Summers out of my mind. I closed my eyes and allowed myself to relax as the hot water hit my body, but it did little good. Ever since running into Brooke this morning at the coffee shop, she was all that had occupied my mind. Truth was, she had been occupying my mind daily for a while now, and after that call, I'd prayed that my new assistant wasn't her. I'd prayed that fate wouldn't be that cruel because I knew I wouldn't be able to keep my hands off her.

She'd been my one and only regret when it had come to the women I had dated. She was the only one I'd wished I'd taken things a little further with. However, by the time I had grown the balls to do so, she'd run off with another man without so much as a backward glance. The night I had applied to Brixton Finance, I'd sent her a message. She was the only person I knew who lived in the area, and I'd immediately messaged her after I'd sent my resume. We'd shared many texts over the course of the last month, but when she'd seen me this morning, she'd looked lost for words. Although, I would have been surprised to see her as well because I had mentioned nothing about possibly moving to New York.

I closed my eyes, her face flashing in my memory. She was still as beautiful as she'd been all those years ago. It was like time had stood still for her. It didn't matter how much time had passed, because as soon as I laid eyes on her, all those thoughts and feeling came rushing back to me. I could still remember the feeling of running my fingers through her long, dark hair and looking into those eyes before kissing her. They still sparkled. Although they weren't sparkling today. Perhaps the man she'd run off with had broken it off with her, or at least I could hope. I shook my head at that thought.

She'd always been someone who had been in reach, but someone that fate wouldn't ever let me touch. The second her eyes had landed on me, the same sexual tension that had always been between us was there. The desire, the want, the need was all wrapped up in one tight little ball and had the potential to be explosive under the right conditions.

I shut the water off and wrapped a towel around my waist. I glanced at my phone, hoping she would have taken the opportunity to message me before now, but she hadn't. I thought back to the first time I'd kissed her. I could still remember it like it was yesterday. I could still feel those soft lips of hers meeting mine, the feel of her hand as she would rest it on my shoulder, and I would be lying to myself if I said I didn't want to feel them again, at least one more time. I just hadn't realized how badly until I'd seen her this morning. I felt my cock twitch at the thought.

I blew out a breath. I needed to get out of this room

and grab some air. I clenched my fists and turned away from the window and was about to grab my phone off the bed when it vibrated. A funny feeling in the pit of my stomach crept through me when I glanced at the screen. With my heart in my throat, I unlocked my phone and answered.

The TV droned on in the background while I sat on the couch staring down at the last text message Nate had sent me. From the second he had left the coffee shop, I hadn't been able to stop thinking about him. I had come home, had a hot shower, and then flopped down on the couch, closing my eyes, trying to clear my mind of him. It had done little good. I read his words over again from the last message he had sent. 'It would be great to see you again' he'd written, which I replied with a smiley face emoji and nothing more. I never thought I'd actually run into him.

I closed my eyes and thought back to the very last night we had spent together. We were home for summer break, my parents had gone away for the weekend, and I had the house to myself. I had called him and invited him over as soon as my parents' car had left the driveway.

"I'll be there in about an hour," he said, his deep, sexy voice sending chills through my body. *"I can't wait to see you."*

"Neither can I," I whispered just as we hung up the phone.

I'd waited almost two hours and still no Nate. This wasn't uncommon, and I saw nothing had changed. He was probably at some party and was taking his time.

I wandered into the kitchen to grab a bottle of wine from the fridge and cracked it open, pouring myself a glass. By the time he had arrived, the bottle was empty, and I was drunk.

He'd been through the door less than five minutes before his arms were wrapped around me and we were on the way down the hall to my bedroom. We'd fallen into my bed and began messing around. The next thing I remembered was waking in the morning, to him lying beside me, wide awake.

"Well, good morning," he murmured.

"What happened?" I questioned, looking around the room and then down at myself, dressed in nothing but a T-shirt that I hadn't remembered putting on. I looked around for my bra and saw it flung neatly over the lampshade by my bed, my panties hung on the back of my desk chair. Horrified, I looked back at Nate, a wry smile on his face. "We

didn't…" I could feel the panic rising in my chest at the thought. *"Did we?"*

"No. We didn't. You passed out." He chuckled.

I blinked hard and opened my eyes, staring at my ceiling. The same feeling I'd felt when I woke up that morning was the same as I was feeling now. Only this time it wasn't a feeling of relief, but one of total regret. How much I hated that bottle of wine I had drunk, and I always wondered what might have happened had I not drank it. Would things have been different? Would we have finally gone all the way that night? I would never know the answer to that. I blew out a breath, sat up, and glanced down at that message again.

My cell phone let out a shrill ring, causing me to jump, and I glanced down at the screen. I swallowed hard when I saw Andrew's name. This was the first time I had heard from him since he had stormed out of the apartment the other night.

"Hello," I answered.

"Hey, how are you."

"Fine. What do you need?" I had to keep myself on edge.

The line was quiet for a minute. "Brooke, I miss you. I made a mistake and I think we should talk about what happened. I want to try and work things out with you. Can I come by tonight?"

God, why did he sound like he was begging, and why suddenly was his voice such a turn-off?

"Please, Brooke."

I glanced around the apartment, and then thought back to Nate and the heat I'd felt when I'd run into him. I wasn't sure I wanted to revisit my relationship with Andrew. I wasn't even sure I loved him.

I tried to search my feelings but realized I was more content being out of this relationship than I ever was in it. I wasn't even heartbroken over what happened between us. Perhaps I needed to sew those oats, I thought to myself.

"Not tonight. Perhaps Monday. It's been a long day on truly little sleep." I said wishing I could just tell him the truth.

The line was quiet, and then I heard him mumble, "Okay. I'll see you then. I'll call you Monday afternoon."

"Okay."

"Oh and, Brooke?"

"Yeah?"

"I love you."

"I'll see you Monday," I murmured and hung up the phone without waiting for a response from him.

I flopped back on the couch and thought about my entire relationship with Andrew. For the first time in a long time, I could finally breathe, and a smile came to my face. I finally felt free. I knew deep down inside that Andrew wasn't the man for me, and I even wondered if I had ever really loved him as anything more than a friend.

I picked up my phone and quickly dialed Andrew back. It was only a matter of seconds before he answered.

"Changed your mind, did you?" He chuckled.

A sudden pang of guilt hit me square in the chest. I closed my eyes and cleared my throat. I had never been the one to end a relationship, and I struggled with what to say. So instead of beating around the fact I didn't want to see him, I decided just to come out and say it. "Andrew, no, I didn't change my mind. I don't want to lead you on to think that more is going to come of us. I don't think meeting you Monday is necessary, I don't think we should see one another anymore."

The line was silent, and I swallowed hard. This had been building inside of me for months, and it had taken the argument the other night to bring it to light.

"Say something," I pleaded.

"Is there someone else, Brooke? Perhaps Frank?" he asked quietly. I could hear the hurt in his voice.

"Frank? As in my old boss?" I asked in shock.

"It's just, since he left, you have been so distracted and distant."

"It's not Frank, Andrew," I muttered with annoyance that he would even suggest such a thing. "I don't want to say no there isn't someone else because I don't know. I just know that this isn't working between us."

The phone was so quiet, I wondered if he had hung up, when I heard him mumble good-bye.

I hung up the phone and walked to the kitchen and poured myself a glass of wine. I drank down half the glass and then refilled it before I returned to the living room. Once there, I picked up my phone and clicked on Nate's contact information, then I relaxed back into the couch cushions.

I glanced at the clock and took a mouthful of wine. With shaking hands, I hit call, then hung up as I felt my chest about to explode with nervousness. I blew out a breath and closed my eyes, trying to build up enough courage. I dialed again, this time allowing the call to go through.

The second it rang, my heart started beating faster, and I fought with myself not to hang up. By the fifth ring, I had convinced myself that I was stupid for even thinking about calling, when I heard his deep voice on the other end of the line. "Hello, Brooke. I was hoping you would call."

The other end of the phone was silent, but if I listened carefully enough, I could make out the sound of her breathing. I smiled to myself. I could remember how she used to talk my ear off endlessly into the night whenever she would call, most nights falling asleep on the phone. Yet, now after a month of texting and flirting, she was suddenly shy.

"I'm glad you called."

"How... How have you been?" I could hear the tremor in her voice and knew instantly that she was nervous, which I found completely adorable.

"Good, you?"

"Not too bad. I didn't catch you at a bad time, did I? I don't want to keep you from anything. I mean, I can let you go."

I silently laughed to myself. "No, Brooke, it's not a bad time. Actually, I was just getting ready to head out for a bite to eat."

"Oh geez, why didn't you say so. I will let you go and call you later."

I laughed aloud. I couldn't help myself. "Are you trying to take back this phone call?"

"No, its just I don't want to bother you."

"Never a bother, actually, I hate eating alone. It would be so nice to have some company." The line was completely silent as I waited for her reply. "Would you care to join me, Brooke?"

Again, there was silence as I waited for her response.

"I...um. I guess I could be persuaded. Where are you going?"

"Johnny's Oyster House. Is that close to where you are?"

"I know exactly where it is. It will probably take me about forty minutes to get there."

"Forty minutes, huh?" I glanced down at my watch noting the time.

"Everywhere in New York takes forty minutes, perhaps longer, especially during rush hour." She giggled.

"All right, how about I call and move my reservation and I will see you there in an hour. Although, if it's easier, I could always come and pick you up."

The line went silent again, and I once again listened hard to see if she was still on the line.

"No, no, that will take twice as long. I'll meet you there."

"All right then, I will see you soon."

The restaurant was packed when I arrived, and I wondered how I would ever find her, but as soon as I walked into the restaurant, my eyes immediately saw her standing off to the side. She wore a tight-fitting black skirt and a button-down sweater that fit her snugly, accentuating all those curves I'd been dying to touch for the last month, even more so now. A white gold necklace sat against the darkness of the sweater, accentuating her slim neck. A neck I immediately wanted to sink my teeth into. I felt my cock stir behind my dress pants as my eyes washed over her body. Hell, I needed to behave myself.

I had just about approached her when she caught sight of me out of the corner of her eye, turned, and smiled gently at me. We weren't even able to get a word in before we were immediately swept off into the restaurant to a table in the back.

After our order had been placed and I had poured wine, we sat there staring at one another. She'd slowly brought her glass to her lips and sipped the cool liquid, looking around the restaurant as if she were uncomfortable, or perhaps looking for someone she knew to save her. "Everything okay?" I asked.

"Yes, of course," she said, giving me a smile.

I leaned across the table and met her eyes. "Do you remember what happened the last time you had wine in my presence?" I couldn't help myself. I wondered if she remembered, and I wanted to break the ice somehow.

Her cheeks flooded with a rush of color and she set her glass down. "Oh my god, I can't believe you actually remember that."

"Of course I do."

"Probably wasn't the best idea I've had."

"It wasn't necessarily a bad idea." I winked.

"Really? Were you even there? I made a complete ass out of myself that night," she whispered, sitting forward. "I can only imagine what you must have thought of me."

"No, you didn't make an ass out of yourself." I

chuckled at the memory. "I never thought bad of you. I do, however, remember how freaked out you were the next morning."

"Yeah, well, I just didn't want to have done something that I didn't remember. Do you know what I mean?"

I nodded. "Understandable, but know that I would never have been one to take advantage of you in a situation like that." I met her eyes.

"I'm glad to know that, most guys would have jumped on the opportunity."

"I'm not most guys, Brooke. I won't lie. It's not like the thought never crossed my mind, but you meant more to me than a quick romp in the sack. If that was what I had of wanted, I would have gotten my way."

"I did?" she asked, shock lining her voice as she stared at the glass that sat in front of her. She looked up at me, and then her eyes dropped to my lips and then met my eyes again.

"Yes, Brooke. You did. Still do."

She sat there pondering my answer for a moment, and then looked at me with a flirtatious glint in her eyes. "Can I ask you a question?"

"Of course."

"Aside from how you apparently felt about me, why

didn't you? I mean, it wasn't like I would have put up a fight."

She was right, she wouldn't have put up a fight. For most guys, she would have been considered an easy target. For, me it wasn't what I wanted for us.

I swallowed hard. "Brooke, I didn't want our first time to be that way." Her head snapped up and she studied my eyes.

"You thought about our first time?" Judging from the look on Brooke's face, she didn't know what to say about that.

"Didn't you?" I asked.

"Well of course, but I never thought you did."

I nodded and swallowed hard. "I'm a guy, Brooke." I shrugged. I had never been so grateful to see our server appear because I could feel myself squirming at my confession. Perhaps it was a little more than I was ready to admit, even to myself. I cleared my throat once the food was placed on the table and the server had stepped away.

"This food looks amazing," Brooke said, taking her napkin and placing it across her lap.

By the time dessert was served, we were back in the same old rhythm we used to have when we were younger. The conversation moved and swayed just like old times. I'd filled her in on what I'd been up to over the past five years. She in turn told me all about Andrew and how things had ended. I'm not going to lie, I was jealous of him.

"So what are you doing in the city?" she asked as she popped the last bite of her food into her mouth.

"I came for a bunch of job interviews, but I got news today that I got one of the jobs I'd applied for, so the search is over."

"That's wonderful. Congratulations. So, you'll be moving here then?"

I nodded. "Yes, within the next couple of weeks."

She smiled. Her blue eyes watched me intently. It was almost like fate was giving us one more chance. One more chance to see where we could take this. I was still as attracted to her as I ever had been—maybe even a little more so—and I personally didn't want this night to end with me kissing her good-bye on the cheek in the doorway of some restaurant and waiting to hear from her.

"So, what are your plans for the rest of the night?" I asked, reaching for the bill and looking at the itemized list.

"I'm going to head home, have a hot shower, and then crawl into bed with a book," she said as she ran her fingers over her necklace and smiled shyly at me.

I could read that flirtatious glimmer in her eyes as

she spoke. I knew that look all too well—the same look she used to give me when she, too, hoped that the night wouldn't end.

"Sounds like a rather lonely way to end the night, Brooke," I said as I popped my credit card into the billfold and set it on the edge of the table.

She cleared her throat and took the last mouthful of wine that was in her glass. "What do I owe you for dinner?" she asked, ignoring my response.

"Not a thing. I got it," I said, tapping the holder and holding it out for the server to take it.

"Are you sure?"

"Yes."

Once the bill had been paid, we walked out of the area to where I had parked my car. I was about to suggest Brooke come with me, but before I could say anything, she walked over to the edge of the road and held her hand out for a cab.

"What are you doing?"

"I'm grabbing a cab. I'd normally just take the subway, but it will probably be busy tonight," she said, trying to wave down another cab that just sped on by.

"Don't be silly. I can give you a lift," I said, nodding towards my car.

"No, it's okay. I don't want to be a care package."

"You aren't. I wouldn't have offered if I didn't want

to." I walked over and placed my hand on her lower back. The second my hand touched her, I felt the bolt of electricity flow up my arm, and I felt her stiffen. "I'll take you," I whispered and slowly directed her towards my car.

"Really Nate, it's fine," she insisted as we were halfway to my car.

"No, don't be silly, I will take you. Better yet, why don't you come back to my hotel and share a congratulatory drink with me in the lounge. Afterward, I'll pay for a cab to take you home."

She looked up at me, fiddling with the handle of her purse. She looked away and then back to me. I could tell she wanted to say yes. She wanted to come back with me, but something was holding her back.

"Just for a drink. One drink," I persisted.

She bit her bottom lip and looked around at the cars driving past. I could tell she was still going over everything in her mind, the way she used to when she was unsure of making the wrong decision. "Okay, one drink. Then I will take a cab home, but I will pay."

"Fair enough," I said, holding up my hands.

I had been on edge throughout the entire dinner, even more so after he'd admitted that he cared about me. I had promised myself when I had taken a breather and slipped into the bathroom during dinner that, as soon as the meal was over, I would get into a cab and head home. Instead, here I was, sitting beside him in his car traveling to his hotel. The scent of his cologne filled the car, and I sat looking out the passenger's side window trying to calm my beating heart.

It felt like the drive was taking forever when, finally, Nate pulled the car into the underground parking lot of The Plaza Hotel and found a parking spot. We took the elevator in silence up to the lobby where we found the lounge had closed early because of a private function. I looked around nervously, unsure what I should do now.

"Well, as lovely as that thought was, I guess I will grab that cab now then," I murmured.

"Nonsense, I'll just order us a drink through room service. If you are okay with coming to my room, that is."

Oh God. I wasn't sure being alone with him was going to be a good idea, but another part of me—the part that always wondered what would have happened between us—screamed at me to go. *I'm supposed to be turning over a new leaf, be more spontaneous, sew oats.* I could hear the words I had spoken to Sara repeat in my mind.

I glanced at my watch to see that it was almost eleven. "Uh, I'm not sure."

"It's a drink, Brooke," he said, placing his hand on my lower back, "If I can't get you a cab later I will drive you back."

I suddenly felt a little silly, smiled at him and followed him over to the front desk where he placed an order for a bottle of wine to be delivered to his room. Then we headed over to the elevator. In a matter of minutes, we were locked in his hotel room. I stayed inside the entryway, afraid to remove my shoes or set my purse down. He had already shed his suit jacket, laying across the back of a chair, and I watched as he loosened his tie and opened the top three buttons of his dress shirt. He turned and unbuttoned and rolled both his sleeves, exposing his strong muscular forearms.

"Are you going to come in and relax or are you going to drink from there?" He chuckled.

I glanced around the room again and nervously toed my shoes off and slowly stepped into the room. I took in a breath and set my clutch down on the table and clasped my hands together. I didn't know whether I should sit or stand and once I had decided a knock on the door caused me to jump.

"That will be the wine," Nate said as he brushed past me to get to the door, leaving a trail of his scent behind.

I couldn't help but check him out as he made his way to the door. He was so fucking attractive, maybe even more so now that he was older. He carried the ice bucket and wine back into the room and quickly opened it, pouring two glasses, then passed one to me.

"To new beginnings," he said, raising his glass.

I brought my glass to his and then took a sip. "To new beginnings," I whispered praying that somehow that toast may have had two meanings.

"Take a seat." Nate nodded to the unused bed. "Relax."

A few sips of wine did wonders to relieve the tension I'd felt building, and finally the conversation began flowing again, as did the wine, and before I knew it, we had polished off the entire bottle. I glanced once again at my watch and saw it was way past midnight.

"I really should get going. It's late, and I am sure you have something you need to do tomorrow," I said, swallowing hard.

I didn't give him a chance to respond. I got up and went over to where my shoe's lay on the floor. I had slipped one foot into my flat when I felt the heat from his body behind me and then felt his hands as they rested on my hips. I closed my eyes and froze as his body got closer to mine. I could feel the pull that had been building between us all night getting stronger the closer he got. When I felt his fiery breath on my earlobe, I turned and met his eyes.

He didn't back away. Instead, he too, looked into mine, the look saying so much. The next thing I knew, I was securely wrapped in his arms in the biggest hug I think anyone had given me. "I've missed you so much," he whispered.

I wrapped my arms tighter around him, hugging him back. Within seconds, the uneasiness that I had felt all night disappeared, and my body relaxed in his arms.

"I missed you to."

He pulled away and looked down into my eyes, and then hugged me again, this time longer and tighter. When we pulled back this time, his eyes washed over my face and my breath hitched. As if in slow motion, he leaned in, with my breath almost choking me, and my heart beating at a pace it should only beat at when running a marathon, he brushed my lips with his. My heart clenched. I found it hard to breathe for the first few seconds, but the instant his lips were gone, my insides were screaming for them to return. He studied my eyes, like he were studying what I had been silently praying for, for years. Even though it felt like forever, almost instantly, his lips were back on mine, and he held me tightly as he kissed me again, deeper this time.

The longer we kissed, the more intense it became, and soon I found myself pressed up against the wall, that dull ache between my legs becoming a throbbing as his muscular hands traveled down my body and rested on my waist. I so desperately wanted him to touch me, for him to quell that ache that had been inside of me. I wanted so badly to be his for just one night, and if one night was all we ever got at least I could say without regret that it was worth it. He pressed me harder up against the wall and kissed my neck, his hands running down and gripping my ass as he sucked my earlobe into his mouth.

The second his lips met mine again, I couldn't help but wonder what I had been missing all these years. He pulled away, put his hand on my cheek and looked into my eyes, and slowly kissed me again.

"I've wanted you all these years," I whispered as I kissed her harder. The want had never dulled, the ache just as strong now as it had been years ago. Finally, she was in my arms, and I wanted to dull this ache I had carried in my soul all this time. I pulled back and looked down at her, and then she wrapped her arms around my neck and pressed her body into mine.

I met her lips again, this time my tongue washing through her mouth. A soft moan escaped her lips, and I felt her slide her fingers into my belt loops. Kissing her harder, I felt her thumb brush the tip of my cock through my pants. My hard, throbbing cock jumped at her soft, faint touch, and now I wanted even more than just a kiss. I wanted her on the bed spread open before me. I gripped her ass and ground myself into her, another soft moan coming from her.

There was no way I was letting this moment pass by. I picked her up and guided her legs so she would wrap them around me, her skirt instantly sliding up around her waist. I could feel the heat from between her legs. I wondered if she was wet for me. If it were possible, I felt my cock get even harder at the thought of wanting to know. I carefully placed her on the bed.

I stood over her, looking down at her, my hand cupping her cheek. I reached down and fiddled with the buttons on her sweater, easily slipping each one open. Once the last button had popped, the sides of the sweater fell away, and I fiddled with the clasp on the front of her bra. Within seconds, I exposed her breasts, her cheeks flushed as she met my eyes. I pushed her back onto the bed and knelt beside her, sucking one of her nipples into my mouth.

She ran her fingers through my hair, gripping a handful as I sucked a little harder. My other hand found its way into her panties, and one swipe through her center told me everything I was dying to know. She was drenched, and the second my finger danced over her clit, she moaned loudly.

She fumbled for the button on my pants. The

second she had flicked it open, I felt the release of pressure as my cock sprung free. I gasped when she wrapped her hand around me and began gently stroking me as I ran my fingers through her hot, wet center again. I pulled my hand from her panties and took my shirt off, allowing it to fall to the floor, and before I could get my hand back where I wanted it, she sat up and took me in her mouth. The second my cock hit the back of her throat, I let out a deep groan, dropped my head back, and laced my fingers through her hair.

I could already feel my orgasm building and had to stop her. I wasn't going to last long if she kept that up, and I didn't want to embarrass myself. When she took her mouth off me, I took her hands and laid her back on the bed, once again kissing her deeply. I unzipped her skirt, kissing her hip, and then pulled both that and her panties off at the same time.

I wanted to be inside of her, if only ever once. I broke our kiss and brushed the hair from her eyes. "I want to feel you," I whispered, kissing her neck.

"I'm on the pill." Her eyes met mine with a pleading look, which made me know that she, too, was feeling the same way I was.

She parted her legs so I could kneel between them,

and I ran my cock through her wet centre. I gave myself a couple of pumps before sliding myself into her, slowly, letting her accommodate me. She was so wet, so tight, that I couldn't keep myself from moaning as I slid into her.

From the second I laid eyes on him in the coffee shop, I had been dying for him to touch me. Then, all night through dinner, the same feelings sat there, every nerve in my body on fire, and I had finally gotten my wish. With every kiss, every touch, every pump, I felt myself getting closer to the brink. When I felt myself tighten around him, that was when he slowed. Long, hard, deep strokes and firm but gentle kisses finally brought me over the edge.

My fingers dug into his back as I felt my orgasm escape me, then he collapsed against me, breathing hard. Kissing me one more time before he pulled himself from inside of me, he then made his way to the bathroom.

I lay there staring up at the ceiling, the commonsense part of my brain waking up, wondering what had just happened between us. When I heard the water run, I sat up and picked my panties and skirt up off the floor. I slipped into them, grabbed my bra and sweater, and had fully dressed by the time Nate returned to the room.

I saw the hint of disappointment in his eyes as he glanced over at me. "Is everything okay?" he questioned, stepping from the bathroom and meeting my eyes.

"Yep, it's just late, and I really need to get home," I mumbled.

I needed to get home before I burst into tears at the thought of what had just happened. Years of pent-up want had hit and allowing the thoughts of possibly never getting to experience that again had me in fight-or-flight. Not only had it been the most intimate experience I'd ever had, but he had kissed and held me like no other man ever had.

"Oh," he said, looking around the room. "Are you okay? I didn't hurt you, did I?"

I swallowed hard and gave my best smile. "No, you didn't hurt me. I'm fine. Why wouldn't I be?" I walked over to where my shoes lay on the floor and slipped them on and then turned to look at him. He met my gaze. I could see he was trying to figure out what had happened in those few quick minutes he had left.

I wasn't even sure what to say. We just stood staring at one another. I was about to turn and walk to the door when he stepped closer and wrapped his arms around me, pulling me against his bare, warm chest for another one of his amazing hugs.

"You are more than welcome to spend the night here," he whispered in my ear.

I hugged him tightly. It was so tempting, wondering what it would be like to wake up to him in the morning, but I didn't want to let my heart to get even more attached to someone I was already very attached to. I thought hard about it but shook my head.

"No, honestly, I think it's for the better that I get home. I don't want to, but I really should." I leaned in and kissed his cheek. "Good night, Nate."

His hand cupped my cheek and, once again, he leaned in and kissed me like I hadn't been kissed before. He was making this harder on me than this should have been.

"You have my number, should you want to stay in touch," he said, running his thumb over my lower lip before placing one last kiss on my lips. "I'm in town until Tuesday morning. Just so you know, I'd like to see where this might go, Brooke."

I nodded, his words almost breaking my heart as I pulled the door open and walked out of Nate's room and into the hall and made my way down to the elevator. I glanced back to see if Nate was in the hallway, but it was empty and his door was shut tight. I pressed the button and waited for the elevator.

I spent the next few minutes fighting with myself, debating whether to turn around and go back or walk away. I wanted to turn around and go back, tell him I wanted the same thing, but I couldn't. I was scared.

When the elevator door opened, instead of turning around, I stepped in, took one more look down the hall toward Nate's room, and hit the button for the lobby.

Brooke

I walked into Better Beans Monday morning and relished in the scent of coffee. My stomach let out a growl. I'd been running late this morning and hadn't taken enough time to eat anything when I spotted Sara standing off to the side.

"Hey, girl. It's about time you got here. I ordered for us already," she said as she shoved her phone into her purse.

"You are a lifesaver. I've been running behind all morning."

"Not really. A mocha latte pusher maybe, but not a life saver," she said, glancing at her watch. "And it's only eight in the morning. Running behind isn't even possible." She laughed out loud.

Ignoring her comment, I looked around the restaurant. "I'll grab us that table over there."

I wandered over to a booth in the back of the little cafe and sat down, Sara following with our order. She sat down across from me and handed me my scone and my latte. "Extra whipped cream?" I asked, taking a sip.

"You know it! So, don't leave me in suspense. Did you talk to Nate? I swear your answer had better be yes because, if you turned down that handsome hunk of a man, there is something definitely wrong with you."

She had no idea, there was something definitely wrong with me. I smiled and nodded. "I did. Saturday night, after I told Andrew I didn't want to see him anymore, I called him."

"You did? And? What happened? Come on, don't leave a girl hanging!"

I laughed out loud at her excitement. "We spent the night together. We had dinner, then we went back to his hotel and one thing led to another."

Sara's jaw dropped at my confession. "Oh my God, you didn't."

I could feel the blush rise to my cheeks. There was nothing wrong with what we had done.

"Yes. I told you I was turning over a new leaf, being more spontaneous."

"...sewing oats." We both said in unison.

Immediately Sara looked serious, "And?"

I was quiet for a moment as I thought to myself. "It was amazing. Honestly, Sara, no one has ever made me feel the way he did. I don't know what else to say. I just know that how he made me feel is how I want to feel every single time."

"Well, girl, I'll give it to you. At least you are going after what you want instead of settling for the next best thing."

"Or I might be stupid."

"What do you mean?"

"I panicked. I hadn't even come down from what had happened between us, and I left. He wanted me to stay, but I couldn't. I left him in his room alone and I walked home."

"Whoa, Brooke."

"Seriously, I was just so overwhelmed that I didn't know how to handle it."

"Have you called him?"

I shook my head. "Not yet. I'm afraid that I may have blown it, plus things seem to be lining up way too easily."

"What like fate is testing you?"

"I don't know, I just know that it just feels like it's too good to be true. Then I wonder what will happen if there is never another who makes me feel that way, and that…" I paused. I didn't know exactly what I wanted to say.

"That what?"

"That perhaps things had never progressed between us in the first place because we weren't meant to be together. Perhaps, he was supposed to stay…forbidden."

The second those words flew from my mouth, I knew I had been right. We were never meant to be because with every touch and every kiss, I knew deep down inside that he was exactly that—forbidden.

"What? What are you talking about? You think that fate tempted you, just to give you a taste of him and then take him away from you again, as some sort of twisted punishment?"

I nodded and took a sip of my latte.

"Girl, you are crazy. Perhaps it's been one-too-many mocha lattes," she said, reaching for my cup, which I pulled out of her reach. "Listen, why don't you reach out to him? Especially if you feel that strongly. Don't make yourself suffer, AGAIN."

"I'll think about it."

"Girl, just do it. What happened to sewing oats and being more spontaneous?"

"Honestly, it doesn't seem to have been that good of an idea."

"Sweets, look, I have to get to the office or my boss is going to be extremely angry. I was late three times last week. Seriously, just text him, something, anything, put yourself—hell, put me out of your misery."

"All right, girl, have a good day," I said, standing up and giving her a hug.

"Oh, have you found out who your new boss is yet?"

I shook my head. "No, but I will be in about ten minutes, which means I, too, need to run. I'll call you after work?"

"Sounds good." We hugged again and then together we headed out the door of Better Beans turning in opposite directions.

I dumped my empty cup into the garbage just outside the doors of one of the tallest buildings in New York. I could feel a nervous energy in the pit of my stomach. I knew that feeling was because my new boss was starting today, and even though I knew he would be more than capable of doing the job, there was always that fear that perhaps I may not be up to his standards.

I pressed the button for the sixty-fifth floor and

watched as the doors closed. Normally, that elevator stopped on every floor, but this morning it shot me straight to the top. I stepped out and glanced over at what used to be Frank's office. The blinds were closed, and so was the door, which was an odd sight for me. Frank never sat with those blinds shut, and that nervous feeling returned, causing my stomach to roll and threaten to expose the contents of my breakfast. Regardless, I made my way to my desk, removing my coat and hanging it on the coat stand in the corner.

I had just sat down and turned on the computer when Melissa, one of the other assistants, came running over. "My God, you are so lucky," she whispered as she leaned across my desk.

"Why is that?" I laughed at her excitement.

"Your new boss. He's a far cry from Frank. Have you met him yet?"

"No, not yet. I was told he would start today but that he would be in meetings for most of the day and that I probably wouldn't get to meet him until later on this afternoon."

"Girl, well, just wait. He is gorgeous," she sang in a high-pitched tone.

"My God, Brooke, you are so lucky," Jenna commented as she walked by. "Isn't she, Melissa?"

I couldn't help but giggle as she continued on her

way as they both fanned themselves.

"Seriously, prepare yourself."

The ping of the elevator made Melissa skitter back to her desk, and I quickly opened my email and began digging into the mess that surely awaited me this morning. I glanced up in time to see five of the executives walk out of the elevator and over to my new boss's door. They knocked and went in, closing the door behind them, and within minutes, I saw them leave, this time with a sixth person with them, but I wasn't able to get a good glimpse of him as they made their way down the hall to the boardroom.

"So have you met him yet?" Sara asked as she shoved the last piece of bruschetta into her mouth.

"Well, I met his hair." I giggled. "That was about the only part of him I saw when he left with the upper executives this morning. They must have been heading for a lunch meeting. However, most of the girls on the floor have met him and say he is gorgeous."

"Sounds like perhaps you and Andrew may have split at a good time," Sara said, giving me the same look she always gave me when we spoke about sexy men. "First Nate, now this guy."

I rolled my eyes. We had a super strict no fraternization policy at work, so no matter how hot the person might have been, there was zero chance of me jumping into bed with the man and screwing up my job. "I don't think so. You know the rules."

"What happened to the girl who just said on Saturday it's time to sew oats? Come on, live a little," she said, shaking me.

I let out a loud laugh and quickly covered my mouth with my hand as people around us looked our way. "Yeah...okay."

My cell phone vibrated on the table, signaling that my lunch break was just about over, and I needed to return to the office. I silenced it quickly and held my hand in the air, signaling for the check.

"You have to go already?" Sara questioned.

"Yeah I'm due back at two," I murmured, sifting through my purse for my wallet.

"Well, don't do anything I wouldn't do and call me after work okay."

"Will do."

I had returned to the office in record time and was behind my desk processing some leftover paperwork from last week when the door to my boss's new office opened. Immediately, a familiar scent hit me. I was surrounded by the scent of Nate's cologne, and it brought me back to the night I'd spent with him only a few nights ago. I closed my eyes. Why did my new boss have to wear the same cologne as Nate, I thought to myself.

I got up from my desk and looked out the window, over the city, while waiting for the documents I had just sent to the printer to print, when I heard someone clear their throat.

"Good afternoon, Brooke. If you have a moment, I'd like to introduce you to your new boss."

I turned to see Ron, Frank's old boss, one of the top executives of the company, standing at my desk. "Good afternoon, Ron. Sounds good." I nodded. "I'll be along in just a minute."

"That's just fine Brooke." He said and took off towards Frank's old office. I waited for the last document to print and then I slowly trailed behind him, reading over the letter that I had just written as I walked. He walked in ahead of me, introducing me to the man I had yet to meet. I glanced up, and when Ron stepped aside, I felt all the blood drain from my face as the man sitting behind the desk looked up at me.

Nate Templeton was my new boss and fate had once again kicked me in the ass.

I felt as if someone had dipped me into a pan of hot oil as I stared into the eyes of the man whose body I had been writhing against less than seventy-two hours earlier. I stood there, not sure what to do. Nate, however, had no problem acting calm. He straightened his tie and held his hand out to me as if we'd never met before.

"Hello, Brooke, I'm Nate. Nice to meet you," he said and waited for me to place my hand in his.

"Brooke was Frank's right hand and probably sometimes his left. She will make sure that your transition is easy, that much I can assure you. Isn't that right, Brooke?"

I almost choked on his words. I knew in my mind that Nate would let me be his right and left hand anytime he wanted, and until three minutes ago, I'd have had no problem with it either. I swallowed hard and nodded.

"I'm sure she will," Nate said, clearing his throat and looking directly into my eyes.

I just stood there, not sure what to do. The tension in this office was almost unbearable, and I hoped that Ron didn't notice it. The company frowned upon this sort of stuff. I was sure Nate would have signed the almost ten-page waiver on it when he had been hired. He had to know that nothing could happen between us now, in or out of the office, no matter how badly either of us wanted it to.

"Well, I will let you the two of you get to work. Nate, I will see you tomorrow morning at the meeting. Brooke, you have a pleasant afternoon."

"Yes. You as well. Thank you." That was all I could manage to say. I glanced to Nate who hadn't taken his eyes off of me and left the room.

I'd bolted from that office and by my desk and ran down to the washroom. I glanced at myself in the mirror. My skin was flushed, and I swallowed hard trying to quell the panic that was rising inside of me. I had to compose myself. I turned the cold water on and soaked a paper towel placing it on the back of my neck. Everything was a mess. I had gotten involved with the man from my past, a man whom I had never really gotten over. My heart and soul knew what it wanted, my conscious said it was wrong, and I was in a state of confusion so great I doubted I would ever have a normal day working beside him.

Once I had calmed down I returned to my desk and put one hundred percent of my attention on my work and worked through the afternoon, ignoring everything else. Nate had tried to get me in his office almost three times within that first hour, but I couldn't. Instead, I'd just reply with an email and the answer to his question.

I worked through the dinner hour, and at seven, I realized I needed a file from Nate's office. Everyone had gone home, Melissa and Jenna had said good night over forty minutes ago, and I was positive Nate had already left. I'd seen him head out of his office at five and hadn't seen him return, so I figured it was safe.

I pulled my hair from the clip I'd had it in and headed to his office in my bare feet. I gently pushed the door open a little and saw an empty desk. Breathing out a sigh of relief, I walked over to the far corner and pulled the filing cabinet drawer open, quickly flipping through the files. The scent of his cologne in the room was distracting at best, and I could already feel a pool of heat growing between my legs. I swallowed hard and forced myself to concentrate on what I was doing. I'd have to get a grip on myself if I was going to be working with him, there was going to be zero room for hormones. The second I found the file I needed, I pulled it from the drawer and was about to turn around when I heard the door click shut behind me.

Startled, I spun around to see Nate standing at the door. He looked good enough to eat. His tie hung loosely around his neck. The white dress shirt he wore was open at the neck, showing off his magnificent chest, and he'd rolled his sleeves up, just like the other night. Our eyes locked for a few seconds, and then I watched as he flipped the lock on the door.

"I um, I thought you'd left," I whispered, swallowing hard as I stood behind his desk watching as he took slow steps toward me. I could see the heat in his look, the want in his eyes as he continued coming closer. I could feel the want building in me which I tried to fight but it did little good.

He shook his head. "I've been thinking of you all day, Brooke. You're consuming my every thought."

"I am?" I asked, shocked at his admission.

He nodded. "You know what I have been thinking of since you walked into my office today?"

I shook my head and bit my lower lip, trying to keep my composure.

"What it would be like to see you in nothing, your

legs spread apart as you sat on the corner of my desk, moaning and begging for me to sink my cock into you while I lick and suck your pussy."

I swallowed hard and let out a slight groan at the thought. I could feel the dull ache I'd had between my legs for most of the afternoon turn into a hard throbbing as he looked at me and I clenched my thighs. It had seemed to take forever for him to reach me, but when he did, his hand came to my cheek. I felt the file slip from my fingers and crash to the floor, papers spilling everywhere. I couldn't say anything. It was like he was reading my mind. Those thoughts were the reason I had stayed hidden behind my desk all afternoon.

I leaned up against the drawer and felt myself slide back as the drawer of the filing cabinet slid back in, Nate was so close to me I could feel the heat from his body as he placed both of his hands on either side of my head.

"I haven't been able to get you out of my mind, Brooke," he whispered, taking his thumb and running it over my bottom lip.

"You haven't," I whispered, swallowing hard.

"No, I haven't," he whispered back, studying my eyes. "Ever since you left my hotel the other night, you have been all I could think about."

"This can't happen here," I whispered, my breathing harsh and heavy as I closed my eyes at the gentleness of his touch.

"I know," he whispered, slowly coming closer, his lips finally crashing into mine. "But I want you so bad." His voice shook as his hands gripped my ass and he pulled me closer into him, allowing me to feel what he'd probably been hiding in his dress pants all afternoon.

I let out a soft moan as he pulled me in tighter, grinding against me.

"I've wanted you all these years, Brooke. Tell me you've wanted me. Tell me that I can finally have you." He moaned as he sucked my earlobe into his mouth.

"I want you," I cried.

He wasted no time. He pulled me over to his desk. The excitement that ran through my veins was almost unbearable. The thought of being caught was beyond thrilling. The sound of his zipper being lowered filled the air, and I was sure that had there been people on the floor, everyone would have heard it. He hiked my skirt up and lifted me, setting me on the corner of his desk.

Kissing me once more, he knelt down, taking my foot and resting it on his shoulder. He pushed my other leg open. I watched the look on his face as he took two fingers and ran them over my soaked panties with just enough pressure for me to feel him.

"So wet," he hissed.

I bit my bottom lip as he continued to run his thumb over my soaked panties. I watched as he licked his lips and swallowed hard. He looked up at me, the intense look in his eyes telling me I was in for it. He pulled my panties to the side and lowered his mouth to me. His tongue ran over and over the small bundle of nerves, causing me to drop my head and a low moan to escape my throat.

"Quiet," he whispered, continuing his torture.

I was just about to scream when he stood up and pulled his cock from his pants, taking it in his hand, and giving it a couple of pumps. I felt the pressure at my opening as he slid into me, his lips meeting mine in time to mute the moan I could feel about to escape. He was relentless as he pumped into me, holding me against him tightly. It didn't take long for me to feel my orgasm building. A few more deep strokes and I felt him stiffen, and we both let go at the same time, clinging to one another.

Breathing hard against one another, he pulled away and looked into my eyes. "I feel like I am finally right where I belong, with you."

I nodded and kissed his lips. "Same here."

"Are we going to make this relationship work?" he asked, kissing me again.

I nodded. "I hope so, but this can't happen at work," I said seriously.

"Really, because that was really hot."

"Yeah, it was, but if you promise to be on your best behaviour here at work, I have an office in my apartment." I giggled as he met my lips.

"Namaste." Every person in the Saturday morning yoga class said in a low voice.

I took a moment to lay back on my yoga mat and look up into the trees. I stretched my arms over my head taking a moment to myself.

"What are you doing?" Sara asked coming to stand over me.

"I'm taking a minute to regroup."

"Regroup? What was the class for then?" She giggled looking down at me.

"I know, I know. It's just I've enjoyed this class more than I usually do. I just feel so at one with everything." I giggled, sitting up and beginning to gather my things and place them into my bag.

"When does Nate get back?"

"Uh tomorrow." I said smiling as I rolled my mat up, thinking of how exciting the last few weeks had been.

"Is this it, will he be here permanently?"

"Yep."

"So, he found a place then?"

"He did." I smiled, still holding onto our secret as I secured my mat with its carry case.

"That's awesome. Did you want to grab a coffee?"

I glanced down at my watch checking the time. "Not sure I can today, perhaps tomorrow?"

"Yeah, I can do tomorrow." Sara said picking up her stuff.

We walked to the edge of the park, hugged, and then went our separate ways. I walked through the streets of New York, excited to get back to my apartment. Nate would be arriving in about thirty minutes, and I didn't want him to arrive to an empty apartment.

I stopped at a flower vendor and grabbed a bunch of sunflowers, quickly paying her and continuing on my way. I'd gotten home, gotten the flowers in water, and had put away my yoga gear when I heard the buzzer.

I ran over and quickly pressed the button, "Come on in." I called.

I opened the door to my apartment and waited, excitement filling me when I heard the ding of the elevator down the hall. It was a matter of moments before Nate stood in front of me, duffel bag flung over his shoulder, looking sexier than ever in a pair of ripped jeans and a black sweater.

"Mover's will be here shortly." He said as he walked in, dropping his duffel bag on the floor, and pulled me into his arms.

I breathed in his scent and relaxed in the comfort of his arms. He was finally mine; we were finally each other's; and we could not wait to embark on our journey together.

About the Author

S.L. Sterling had been an avid reader since she was a child, often found getting lost in books. Today if she isn't writing or plotting, she can be found buried in a romance novel. S.L. Sterling lives with her husband and dog in Northern Ontario.

Want to stay in touch?

Sign up for my weekly Newsletter.

Join my Reader Group
Sterlings Silver Sapphires

Or

Visit my Website

Other Titles by S.L. Sterling

It Was Always You

On A Silent Night

Bad Company

Back to You this Christmas

Fireside Love

Holiday Wishes

Saviour Boy

The Boy Under the Gazebo

Into the Sunset

The Greatest Gift

The Malone Brother Series

A Kiss Beneath the Stars

In Your Arms

His to Hold

Finding Forever with You

Vegas MMA

Dagger

KB Worlds

Constraint

Willow Valley

Memories of the Past

The Holiday Dilemma

Letters from the Heart

Doctors of Eastport General

Doctor Desire

The Spencer Brooks Diaries

Our Little Secret

Our Little Surprise

Our Little Wedding